The Smallest Horse
in the World

by

Jeremy Strong

Illustrated by Scoular Anderson

You do not need to read this page –
just get on with the book!

First published in 2006 in Great Britain by
Barrington Stoke Ltd
www.barringtonstoke.co.uk

This edition based on *The Smallest Horse in the World*,
published by Barrington Stoke in 2005

ISBN 1-842994-11-5
13 digit ISBN 978-1-84299-411-5

Printed in Great Britain by Bell & Bain Ltd

Meet The Author – Jeremy Strong

What is your favourite animal?
A cat
What is your favourite boy's name?
Magnus Pinchbottom
What is your favourite girl's name?
Wobbly Wendy
What is your favourite food?
Chicken Kiev (I love garlic)
What is your favourite music?
Soft
What is your favourite hobby?
Sleeping

Meet The Illustrator – Scoular Anderson

What is your favourite animal?
Humorous dogs
What is your favourite boy's name?
Orlando
What is your favourite girl's name?
Esmerelda
What is your favourite food?
Garlicky, tomatoey pasta
What is your favourite music?
Big orchestras
What is your favourite hobby?
Long walks

This is for Bella who likes animals
(and strawberries) of all sizes

Contents

Chapter 1
Swan

Bella had a problem with the new girl in her class. She was called Swan. It was a nice name for a girl. But the problem was this. Swan wasn't nice and Bella didn't like her.

Swan hadn't been at the school long and she was hard to like. She was a show-off. She was rude and loud and big and bossy. She was always telling everyone how rich her parents were.

"They've got millions," she said on her first day at school.

"They've got billions," she said on the second day. And so it went on. Bella got the feeling that Swan was lying.

"You're making it all up – about your parents being so rich," Bella said, in front of everyone.

Swan looked at Bella hard. Bella could see she was very angry. Swan stuck her hands on her hips, came up to Bella and stood very close.

"I am NOT making it up," Swan said crossly. "My parents are rich, rich, rich. They've got two big posh cars and a helicopter. So there."

Bella stepped back. Swan was a big girl, and Bella wasn't. "Well," Bella went on, "I don't think it's true. And you've got a silly name."

But Swan wasn't a silly name. Bella wished she hadn't said that, but she had, and now it was too late. In fact, she loved the name. She wished she was called Swan. Bella was angry that a big, lumpy girl could be given such a nice name.

"I've got a funny name, have I?" snapped Swan. "What about yours, Belly?" The other children began to laugh.

"Belly!" they giggled.

"Smelly Belly!" Swan yelled with glee, and everyone laughed some more.

Bella felt her face go hot. She felt angry. She couldn't think of a clever reply. She just stood there for a moment. Then she ran off.

"Jelly Belly!" Swan yelled after her.

For the rest of the school day Bella stayed as far away from Swan as she could. At the end of the afternoon she went out to Mum's car and got in fast. She didn't say a word all the way home. Mum could see Bella was upset but she didn't ask why. Ever since Bella's mum and dad had split up Bella hadn't said much.

I wish I could help Bella – but she wont say what's wrong

When they got home Bella ran to her room and lay on the bed. She looked hard at the floor. Then, she looked hard at the wall. *School was horrible,* she thought. *And Swan was more than horrible.* Bella looked over to the picture by her little desk. She loved that picture. *What would it be like to be inside the picture?* It was of a white horse, galloping in the waves that crashed onto a sandy beach. You could almost feel the spray and smell the salt wind.

Bella went and stood in front of the picture. She wanted to get as close to it as she could. She could even *feel* the wind blowing on her face.

She lifted the picture off the wall. She didn't know it was so heavy. So heavy that she dropped it. It crashed onto her desk. *BANG!*

The glass broke into tiny bits.

As it did so, water and sand rushed out over Bella's desk, and fell onto the carpet below.

And Bella saw the white horse standing there, on her desk, shaking its mane at her. A perfect little white horse, that was only the size of a small kitten.

Chapter 2
Astra

Bella was amazed. She was even more amazed when the horse looked up at her and spoke.

"Have you seen Rufus?" The horse's voice was soft and sweet.

"Rufus?" Bella asked.

"He's my rider," the horse told her. "I've been looking everywhere for him. I lost him

in the battle. I'm not sure how and when."
The horse looked sad. "Maybe he was
killed," the little horse went on. "I hope not.
We've been together for years. He's a good
rider and always kind to me."

The horse stopped and looked round the
room. She saw that this was somewhere
new. She gave a little whinny. This was all
very odd. Bella thought it was odd, too.
They looked at each other, both feeling shy.
Then they both smiled. Can horses smile?
This one could.

"I'm called Astra," said the horse.

"And my name's Bella. This is my
bedroom."

"Oh dear," said Astra, softly. "Now I'm
well and truly lost. You see how small I am
in your world? I must get back into the

world I came from. Then I shall be the right size and I might be able to find my rider, Rufus. I won't find him here."

Bella looked down at the floor, at the water and the sand that had spilt out of the picture. "I can't put the picture back together," she said. "I'm so sorry."

"Then I'll never find Rufus again," said Astra, sadly.

Bella didn't know what to say. But she knew she had to tidy up the mess on the floor. Should she tell Mum about Astra? She went to the door. What would Mum say? She would think Bella had made it all up. About this tiny horse. How could it be true? Bella went to get a dust-pan and brush to sweep up all the sand and broken glass. She looked back at Astra, who was standing on her desk. Then Astra lifted her tail.

"No!" cried Bella, but it was too late. Astra did what horses do, even very small horses. Now Bella had horse poo to clean up, too. Keeping a horse in her bedroom was not going to be all that easy.

Chapter 3

No roses in the bedroom, please

Bella found out a lot of things about Astra that evening. She found out that Astra liked eating straw and sugar lumps and apples. Astra also liked Bella's felt-tip pens – the fruity ones. The felt-tips left bright marks all over Astra's mouth. Bella had to wash them off.

After that, Bella put Astra on the floor. The horse couldn't do much harm there. But Astra loved the straw rug beside Bella's bed. She ate a big lump off the corner. Then she did another poo. Bella seemed to spend all her time brushing up the mess.

"Where are you going?" asked Mum, as Bella dashed past.

"I spilled something," Bella yelled and ran back upstairs. Her room smelt awful. "Oh yuk," she said.

Astra was rushing round and round the little bedroom.

"What's that noise?" Mum called up the stairs.

"It's me. I'm tap-dancing," Bella called back.

"But you don't know how to do tap-dancing, darling."

"I'm just trying it out," Bella called back. She hissed at Astra. "Can't you make a bit less noise? I've got to keep you a secret. If Mum finds out she'll ... she'll send you to a Home for Very Small Horses," Bella giggled. It was all very silly, and great fun.

At last Astra settled down. Bella made her a stable for the night in the front room of her old dolls' house. She put in some straw from the rabbit's hutch and some bits of carrot too. "And if you want to go, please go in the corner," she told the horse.

"If I want to go? What do you mean?" asked Astra.

"You know – *go*."

"I can't *go*. You've shut the door," Astra said.

"I don't mean that kind of go. I mean **go**."

The horse was very puzzled by now. "What kind of go is **go**?" she asked. Bella put her mouth very close to Astra's ear and said something softly.

"Oh!" said Astra. "But horse poo is very good for the roses."

"Roses don't grow in my bedroom," Bella told her.

"They might if I **go** lots," Astra said.

"NO!" said Bella. "They won't! Roses grow in gardens. Now please go to sleep."

For a bit there was no sound. Then Astra spoke. "Do you think I shall ever find Rufus?"

"I hope so," said Bella. But she didn't see how she could help.

"What will happen in the morning?" asked Astra.

Bella opened her eyes! That was a good question. She had school the next day. Mum would be out at work so that would be OK, but would Astra be safe, left alone in the house?

This is a dream come true!

Chapter 4
More trouble with Swan

In the morning Bella was glad to find that Astra had been asleep all night and there was no more mess. Bella gazed down at the sleepy white horse. She had never seen such a perfect little animal. She wanted to stay with Astra, but she had to have breakfast with Mum and go to school.

It was very hard to sit at the table and get on with her breakfast. Bella was longing to tell Mum about Astra, but she knew Mum would think she'd made it all up. And if Mum ever did find Astra, Bella knew she would say there was no way Bella could keep a little horse in her bedroom – most of all one that did poos all over the place.

So Bella tried to keep still and eat her breakfast as fast as she could. "You're in a hurry today," Mum said. "Are you looking forward to school?"

"Yes!" Bella said with a big smile but inside her heart had begun to thump. She had just remembered that someone was waiting for her at school. Swan. Swan and all the other girls who had laughed at her yesterday.

Bella made sure Astra was safe in her room and told the horse to be good.

"I'm always good," said Astra, rather cross. "I only do what all horses do."

"Horses don't eat felt-tips," Bella told her.

"But they smelt so nice," Astra replied.

"Now, be good!" She shut the door.

At school Swan was there in the playground, as she always was. "My dad's going to get us a swimming pool," she told everyone. "It's going to have water slides and real fish, too."

"Wow!" the other girls all said.

"Yeah, and, AND it's going to have not just fish, but dolphins as well."

"Dolphins! That is so cool!" everyone cried.

"Yeah," nodded Swan. "Dolphins and hippos."

Bella was amazed. All the other children seemed to think this was true. But it was crazy. Something inside her snapped.

"That's rubbish," said Bella.

"Oh look, it's Smelly Belly again," said Swan, with a mean look. "It's not rubbish. We're getting a swimming pool."

"You're not going to have dolphins and hippos. I don't think your parents are rich at all. You're just making it all up."

Swan was very angry. She seemed to swell up and get even bigger. Her face went very red. "Oh, yes we are. We're richer than all of you lot! My dad's always buying me things. He's just got me a pony."

"No, he didn't!" shouted Bella.

"He did! And he's brown with a black tail."

The two girls looked hard at each other. Then Bella cracked. "Well, I don't care if he did. I've got my own horse at home, so there."

The other children gazed at her. They had known Bella for ages. "No, you haven't, Bella. You haven't got a horse."

"Yes, I have."

"You can't have one," said Swan, "because girls don't ride horses, they ride ponies."

"It's a horse," Bella told her.

"OK," said Swan. "Show us then. Bring your horse to school tomorrow."

For the first time in ages Bella felt happy. She smiled. "All right," she said, "I will. And Swan can bring in her pony, too."

Bella walked off, but as she went she saw Swan's face and in Swan's eyes she saw ... WILD PANIC.

Chapter 5
Astra goes to school

"Don't you think the house smells a bit?" asked Mum, as she opened the front door that evening.

"Not much," Bella said but she knew Mum was right.

"It does. It smells like a stable in here. How long is it since you cleaned out the rabbits?"

"Oh! Yes, it could be that," said Bella. "I'll clean them this evening." Then she ran upstairs and slowly opened the door to her room. As soon as she did Astra came galloping across the room towards her – clump, clumpety-clump, clump.

"Ssh!" Bella told her. "Mum will hear you."

"Did you find Rufus?" asked Astra. "Did you find him?"

"No," said Bella. "I'm sorry. I don't even know where to look for him." She sat down on her bed. "Mum says the house smells like a stable, and it does, too."

"I like it," Astra said happily.

"That's because you're a horse. It's not the kind of smell humans like."

"Rufus didn't mind."

Bella gazed at the little horse. Who were they, Rufus and Astra? "Where do you come from?" she asked Astra.

"We were fighting the Romans," Astra said.

"The Romans? But that was 2,000 years ago!"

"I don't know when it was, but there was a big battle. We were winning and then suddenly the Roman horse-men attacked us from behind. Somehow Rufus fell off my back but I kept going. I ran far away from the battle. I went back much later when the battle was over and the Romans had gone. It was horrible. There were so many dead bodies. But I couldn't find Rufus. That's why I think he must still be alive."

"But he couldn't be alive now," Bella said. "The battle was 2,000 years ago. Rufus could not be alive now even if he didn't die in the battle."

Astra shook her head. Her eyes shone. "I'm alive," she said. "And I think Rufus could be, too. So where do we start looking?"

Bella had to admit that Astra was brave. And she was not going to give up. How could she help her? She was going to take Astra to school the next day to show Swan. She could begin the hunt for Rufus there. Why not?

Next morning Bella put Astra into her school bag and off they both went. Bella was feeling good as she set off. She didn't care about Swan any longer. She didn't even care if Swan did bring a pony to school. But she knew Swan hadn't got one. Bella had Astra in her bag and that was all she needed.

"It's Smelly Jelly Belly!" Swan shouted as soon as she saw Bella in the playground. "Where's your horse? Ha! You haven't got one!" Swan turned to the others. She looked very smug. "Belly hasn't got a horse! Belly hasn't got a horse!" she sang.

"Where's your pony?" Bella asked. "You were going to bring *your* pony."

"Well, I couldn't. Dad wouldn't let me. He said you can't take ponies to school."

"You haven't got a pony," Bella said.

"Have, have, so there. He's called ... Black Beauty."

"You said your pony was brown," said Bella.

"Never did!" Swan shouted.

The crowd of children began to mutter. "You did, Swan. You said he was brown with a black tail."

Swan went red. "Well, I forgot. His name's Brown Beauty."

"You haven't got a pony," Bella said again.

"And you haven't got a horse!" yelled Swan.

Bella slowly opened her bag. Everyone was looking at her. She put both her hands into her bag and lifted Astra out. She put Astra down in the playground. Astra lifted her head. She snorted and shook her mane. Then she began to gallop round Bella's feet.

The children just stood there and gazed at Astra.

"Oh, wow!" said one at last. "It's a horse. A tiny horse!"

There was a dull thud. Swan lay on the ground in a heap. She'd fainted from the shock.

Chapter 6
Trouble

Bella ran over to Swan and helped her sit up. "Are you all right?"

"I saw a tiny horse," said Swan. "But it's not true, is it? It's some kind of trick."

"It is true. The horse's name is Astra. She fell out of a picture at my house."

Swan tried to smile and stood up slowly. "*My* pony gallops ..." she began, but she didn't finish. Her mouth shut and she gave a long sigh.

Bella was feeling sorry for Swan. It must feel horrible to tell all those lies and then be found out. Bella began to think that Swan didn't look quite so big after all.

"It's OK," Bella said. "I know you never had a pony."

Swan didn't say a word. They watched Astra galloping round, jumping over the children's feet. The children were laughing. Swan gave another long sigh.

"I wish I did have a pony. I wish I had ..." Swan spoke so softly Bella could hardly hear her, "a dad."

Bella gazed at Swan. So Swan didn't have a dad! "My dad doesn't live at home either," she said. The two girls looked at each other.

At that moment the bell went and it was time to go into school. Bella called Astra, picked her up and put her back in her bag. What was going to happen next?

"They don't let you bring horses to school," said one girl, Rose. "They'll be cross with all of us when they find out."

"Well, we'll just have to keep Astra a secret. You know what teachers are like. They'll take her from us if they find out."

"And make her into dog food," added Martin, who loved to tease. "A very small tin of dog food, because she's a very small horse."

"You're stupid," Swan snapped back at him.

"And you're ... umm, bigger than me," said Martin with a grin.

Bella told everyone about Astra's hunt for Rufus. They asked what Rufus looked like. Bella didn't know. Was Rufus a small man, just like Astra was a small horse?

"I only know that he was fighting the Romans," she said.

Swan nodded. "Maybe he came from the Iron Age. They fought the Romans," she said. "They wore cloaks and leggings."

"Yeah, and they all had long hair and huge big beards," Martin added. "And they smelt."

"Martin!" they all shouted.

Bella tried to make them all stay calm. "We must try and find Rufus. We must look out for him all the time."

"In the classroom," said Swan.

"Up the shops," added Rose.

"Down the toilet," Martin said with a grin.

"MARTIN!" they all shouted, and then went into school.

At first it was all fine. Astra kept very still inside Bella's school bag. But she became more and more restless. She wanted to get on with the hunt for Rufus. Astra gave a soft whinny. Bella didn't hear her. So Astra whinnied again, more loudly this time.

"Sssh," said Bella, and there was silence for a bit.

Then – neee-hee-heee-harr!!! Astra was at it again.

The teacher, Mr Frost, jumped from his chair and gazed angrily at the class. He looked at each child in turn. When he got to Bella, Mr Frost stopped. He looked hard at her. Bella had one hand in her bag.

"Bella! WHAT are you doing? Bring your bag here at once."

"But I haven't ..."

"Don't argue, girl. Just bring your bag here at once."

Chapter 7

Swan wants to be a horse

Bella stood up. She lifted the bag from the back of her chair and began to walk up to Mr Frost. At that same moment someone pushed past her.

"It was me, Mr Frost!" cried Swan. "It was me! I made that funny noise! Neee-hurrr!!!! I was being a horse."

Mr Frost looked at Swan. What an odd girl she was.

"Why?" he asked.

"I like horses," Swan told him. "And I want to be one when I grow up." The class began to laugh.

"You want to be a horse when you grow up?" said Mr Frost.

"Yes. A white one."

Mr Frost gazed at Swan. What a very, very odd child.

"Go back and sit down, both of you. Swan, please save your horse noises for the playground."

Bella smiled at Swan as they went back to their seats. Wow, that had been a close one. And then, as Bella got to her table, the strap of her bag got hooked up on the back of Martin's chair. The bag fell on the floor with a thump.

There was a loud, angry whinny from Astra and a moment later she jumped out of the bag. Then she set off at top speed across the classroom floor, galloped out of the classroom door and was gone.

Mr Frost stood up. He was gazing after Astra as she galloped out of the room. "What was that?" he wanted to know.

"A dog!"

"A rabbit!"

"A hedgehog!" This came from Martin.

"A *white* hedgehog?" Mr Frost said crossly.

"So you can't see it when it snows," nodded Martin.

Mr Frost pushed his way past the children. "Stay here while I go after that animal. If I find that one of you has got a dog in school then that child will be punished."

The class watched as Mr Frost went off. They all felt very upset. "We've got to find Astra before he does," Bella hissed.

The children crept out of the classroom and into the hall. They looked everywhere, not making a sound. But all at once the hall was full of other people shouting.

"There's a cat in here!" said Miss Mousetail as she came out of her classroom with all her children behind her.

"Help! It's a badger!" cried another teacher. She stood on her desk and waved a ruler. All her class got up onto their desks, too.

"I saw a tiger!" yelled someone from Year 1.

Then Bella heard the sound she most feared. Mr Frost was yelling louder than all the rest.

"Over here! It's over here!"

Everyone rushed up to Mr Frost. Bella and Swan were right in front. Everyone was gazing down at the floor by Mr Frost's big feet. There, in the middle of the floor was ...

... Phew! At least it wasn't Astra. But it was something Astra had done.

Mr Frost looked at Swan and Bella. He was very angry and his face was very red.

"Well?" he said. "Are you two girls going to explain this?"

Chapter 8
Miss Snow

Bella said nothing. She didn't know what Mr Frost wanted her to explain.

Swan slipped her hand into Bella's.

"It's that animal that one of you had in class just now, isn't it?" Mr Frost said. "I know you're both in this together. Just what kind of animal is it? I want to know at once."

Bella bit her lip. She badly wanted to keep her secret, but she needed to know where the little horse was.

"If you won't tell me what this is all about, then you shall have to tell the head teacher," snapped Mr Frost. "Then you can come back here and clean up the floor."

The head teacher, Miss Snow, was not as bad as Mr Frost, but it was not at all nice to stand in front of her and get told off.

"Oh dear," said Miss Snow, when she heard the story. "Oh dear, dear, dear. You can't bring animals into school. Oh no, no, no. Rabbits in the classroom? No, no, no, no."

How many times would Miss Snow go on saying the same thing again and again?

Bella started gazing at the picture behind Miss Snow's desk, and the more she looked at it the more ... yes, it must be. She winked at Swan and looked up towards the picture. Swan looked up too. Her eyes grew big and she nodded back at Bella.

The picture was of a man who was standing near the edge of a cliff. He was looking out over a sandy beach and the huge waves crashing down on it. His cloak was blowing about in the sea wind. His hand was up by his eyes, as if he was looking for something.

At that moment Bella saw something else. Astra.

The little horse was right by Miss Snow's feet. She was eating the straw mat on the floor. Bella tried to make Astra look at her, but the horse was far too busy eating the mat.

Then Astra found the end of Miss Snow's shoelaces and began to eat those. Swan had seen her, too. But there was nothing the girls could do. They watched as Astra ate the shoelace. It got smaller and smaller until the horse was having to tug at it to eat more.

Miss Snow felt the little tug. She moved her foot away and looked down.

"Oh! Oh oh oh oh oh! A huge white rat! Oh no no no no no!" Miss Snow hopped onto her chair and then onto the desk. Then she jumped down and ran out of the room.

"Quick!" cried Bella to Swan. "Get the painting!" Then she dived under Miss Snow's desk and grabbed Astra. Swan lifted the picture off the wall.

They could hear loud shouts coming from the hall. A gang of teachers were running towards Miss Snow's room.

"It was a huge white rat!" Miss Snow said. "It tried to eat my foot!"

"Don't worry. We'll soon have it!" shouted Mr Frost. "Come on everyone!"

"Quick!" cried Bella. "Hurry up!" The voices grew louder, closer and closer.

Swan held onto the picture and began to open the back. Bella stood beside her, with Astra in her arms. As Swan opened the

picture frame they could smell the sea and a salty wind blew across the room. "Astra, get inside quick! Get inside the picture!"

Astra put two legs inside and sighed. "Rufus!" she said. She turned back to the girls. "Thank you," she said softly. Her eyes were shining.

"Just go!" cried Bella. "Hurry!"

Astra stepped into the picture. For a few moments the whole room seemed to fill with wind, sand, sea and sky. Then the picture snapped shut again. The girls put it back on the wall just in time. A gang of angry teachers rushed into the room.

After that everything was a mess. There was a lot of shouting and running about while the teachers went on looking for a rat that wasn't there!

At last everyone stopped shouting and rushing about. Miss Snow came back into her office. She looked very upset. She looked hard at the picture on the wall. "I know there was a man in that picture. Hmmm. Very odd, very odd indeed. Odd."

Then Miss Snow looked hard at the two girls. They got a good telling off, but they didn't care. Astra was safe with Rufus. And now the odd animal had gone and things at school soon went back to normal.

Swan and Bella went back to the hall and told the class the whole story. Everyone was glad the fuss was over but a bit sad that they no longer had a little white horse to make life more fun for them.

Bella was sorry, too. It had been such fun to have Astra in the house, and at

school, too. Now she was back on her own again, or was she?

No, she wasn't. Swan was still holding hands with her.

If you loved this story, why don't you read ...

SWOP!

by Hilary McKay

Emily loves swops. She even swops her grandmother for a donkey! But will her swops help Emily and her brother escape from their wicked old Aunty Bess?

4u2read.ok!

You can order this book directly from our website
www.barringtonstoke.co.uk

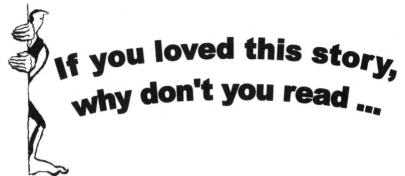

If you loved this story, why don't you read ...

Robin Hood
All At Sea

by Jan Mark

Robin Hood is Britain's **MOST WANTED** outlaw. He robs the rich and gives to the poor – but he's bored of all that! He sets off to sea to begin a new life. But life at sea isn't all plain sailing ...

4u2read.ok!

You can order this book directly from our website
www.barringtonstoke.co.uk